Can the team track down a valuable heirloom?

Hector headed for the memento table. "I want to see if the book is still glow—hey! Jamal!"

"Don't yell, I can hear," Jamal said. "What's up?"

"Did you—um—do some rearranging while we weren't looking?"

"Of course not," Jamal said. He tacked the crepe across the wall behind the couch with tape. Alex held the other end.

"Then somebody is not being funny around here." Hector ran his hand across the empty space on the coffee table.

Tina stopped arranging plastic knives and forks on the dinner table and came over. Lenni followed her.

Lenni gasped. "Gone," she said. "The book is gone!"

The
BOOK

CHASE

by Jacqueline Woodson

illustrations by Steve Cieslawski

A Children's Television Workshop Book

BANTAM BOOKS

NEW YORK • TORONTO • LONDON • SYDNEY • AUCKLAND

THE BOOK CHASE
A Bantam Book / September 1994

Ghostwriter, **Ghost** and ◉ are
trademarks of Children's Television Workshop.
All rights reserved. Used under authorization.
Art direction by Mary Sarah Quinn
Cover design by Susan Herr
Interior illustrations by Steve Cieslawski

For information address: Bantam Books

ISBN 0-553-48190-8

Published simultaneously in the United States and Canada

Bantam Books are published by Bantam Books, a division of Bantam
Doubleday Dell Publishing Group, Inc. Its trademark, consisting of the
words "Bantam Books" and the portrayal of a rooster, is registered in
U.S. Patent and Trademark Office and in other countries. Marca Regis-
trada. Bantam Books, 1540 Broadway, New York, New York 10036.

OPM   0   9   8   7   6   5   4   3   2   1

Chapter 1

"How about these, Grandma CeCe?" nine-year-old Casey Austin asked, holding up a set of Kwanza candles.

Her grandmother smiled but Jamal shook his head.

"No way!" Jamal said. His cousin Casey was spending part of the summer with them. He liked her, but sometimes she could be kind of a pain. Like now. She kept coming up with the dumbest ideas.

Jamal and Casey had been raking through the basement for hours, trying to find old family treasures to display at the upcoming family reunion. Grandma CeCe was helping them look—when she wasn't running upstairs to answer the phone or taste something that was bubbling away in the kitchen. She had just discovered her great-grandmother's embroidered linen tablecloth. Jamal was busily removing the dust from a trumpet that had belonged to his and Casey's great-grandfather.

"But these lights have history," Casey said. "They're from the first time I visited here for the holidays."

"That was only three years ago," Jamal reminded her. "We need *really* old stuff."

Grandma CeCe nodded. "Everyone will be excited to see things they haven't seen in years, things that tell them something about our family history from way, way back." She dug quickly through a box at her feet. "But we have to hurry, you two!"

"*I'm* part of the family history, too, even if I'm not all old and musty and dusty," Casey grumbled. But she dropped the candles back into a box filled with holiday ornaments. Then she continued to rummage through the basement. Jamal smiled.

RING!

"Drat that phone," Grandma CeCe grumbled, climbing to her feet. "It's been ringing off the hook all day."

"Want me to get it?" Jamal offered.

"Thanks, sugar, but no," Grandma said with a sigh. "It's for me. Probably your father asking what kind of lettuce to buy—again." She started up the basement stairs. "All this up and down, up and down! I wasn't built for speed," she muttered.

Casey giggled. Grandma was usually a calm, cool person. But putting the reunion together had made her get pretty rattled.

Just then a glowing, sparkling ball of light zipped past Casey, brightening up the gloomy basement. She turned to Jamal. Her eyes were wide with excitement. "Ghostwriter's here!" she whispered. "Did you see?"

Jamal nodded. He looked excited too.

Jamal was the first person who had seen Ghostwriter. One day a mysterious being had started sending messages to Jamal on his computer. Then he wrote messages to Jamal's classmate, Lenni Frazier, in her songbook. Jamal and Lenni learned that he was a ghost who could communicate only by writing. So they named their strange pen pal Ghostwriter.

Next Ghostwriter communicated with Alex and Gaby Fernandez, then Rob Baker, then Hector Carrero, and finally Casey. The friends were all part of the Ghostwriter team. None of them knew exactly why Ghostwriter had chosen them. But they did know that he was a good friend, someone they could always count on.

"Look!" Jamal said. Ghostwriter's glow was turning deep red. It hung in the air over a pile of yellowed newspapers. Then it dove in.

"What's he doing?" Casey breathed.

A second later the glow shot out of the papers. It was now a bright, pulsing purple.

"He's really excited about something," Jamal said. "What's in those papers?"

Casey was already digging through the pile. In another second she pulled out a small, old, leather-bound book. Dust and bits of paper scattered. Ghostwriter dove into the book, then out again. Three exclamation marks rose up into the air from the newspapers and hung there.

!!!

Jamal frowned. "It just looks like some old book," he said. "Maybe somebody forgot to return it to the library."

Casey brushed some dust from the top. "*Narrative of the Life of Frederick Douglass*," she read slowly.

"My goodness!" Grandma CeCe's voice came from the top of the stairs. She came down them quickly. "Frederick Douglass! Bring that over here, Casey."

Casey's heart skipped a beat. Then she remembered that Grandma couldn't see Ghostwriter. No one except the team could.

She brought the book over. Grandma took it and sat down on a milk crate. "Will you look at this?" she said excitedly. "I clean forgot I had this old book. It's a first edition, you know. It's rare!"

Casey peered over Grandma's shoulder. "Frederick Douglass was a slave, right? We read about him."

"He escaped," Jamal jumped in. "Then he became a speaker and abolitionist."

"What's an a-bol . . . lit . . . ?" Casey asked.

"It's a person who's against slavery," Jamal answered. "Why do we have this book? Is he related to us, Grandma?"

Grandma CeCe shook her head. "Not that I know of. I'm not sure how we got hold of a first edition. All I know is, your Great-Great-Aunt Estelle passed it down to me."

Casey made a face. Aunt Estelle was the crabbiest woman she had ever met. She couldn't believe they were even related. She remembered Aunt Estelle coming to Detroit to visit once, when she was five, and complaining all the time about the way Casey's mother cooked. Casey wasn't looking forward to seeing Aunt Estelle at the reunion.

"Estelle made a big point of telling me to keep this book in a safe place," Grandma CeCe continued.

"Is it worth a lot of money?" Jamal asked.

"Probably," Grandma said. "But it's also full of history about everyone in our family. Look at this letter." She pulled a yellowing piece of paper from between the first two pages. The words on it were so faded Jamal could barely make them out in the dim basement light. He read the first few lines aloud, figuring out the abbreviations as he went.

My dearest Beatrice,
Thank you for yr letter. I am keeping well though on Thsdy. last (20th Jnry.) I had a touch of the grippe.

"What's the grippe?" Casey interrupted. "And why does the writing sound so funny?"

" 'I am keeping well,' " Jamal repeated. "It sounds like the writer is afraid he's going to turn moldy."

Casey giggled. "Pretty good, Jamal—for you."

" 'In this dim light and on the pitching sea my quill moves carelessly across the page,' " Jamal read on. " 'A vision of yr. loveliness is with me always—' "

"Cor-*ny*!" Casey snickered.

"That's probably where you get *your* corniness, Casey," Grandma CeCe told her with a smile. "That letter is from my Grandpa Darden to my grandma." Her thoughts seemed far off as she folded the letter carefully and placed it back inside the book. "I never met him, but I hear tell he was a very impressive man. Grandma Beatrice always referred to him as 'Mr. Darden.' Isn't that something? Calling your own husband 'Mister.' "

"How come he wrote with all those funny abbreviations?" Jamal wanted to know.

"Lord, I don't know," Grandma said. "He was—"

"Grandma!" Jamal's older sister Danitra called down the stairs. "I got all the flowers. Where do you want me to put them?"

"Put a bunch in that vase on the coffee table, and, let's see. . . . " Grandma handed the old book to Casey and walked up the first few steps to talk to Danitra.

Casey held the book in her lap and carefully turned the pages. There were lots of stray papers pressed into the book. All were yellow with age. "Are these all letters, Grandma?" she asked when Grandma CeCe came back down the steps. "They look like they'll fall apart if you touch them. Who put them in there?"

"Estelle, mostly," Grandma explained. "I put a few things in there, too. But Estelle's really the one who saved up most of the bits of history about this family. This book probably holds everything you'd ever want to know about your relatives. Plus it's the story of Frederick Douglass! So it's really two books in one."

"How come Aunt Estelle put everything in this book?" Jamal asked.

Grandma shrugged. "Why don't you ask her?"

"I know why!" Casey said excitedly. "It's because we're really related to Frederick Douglass, isn't it? He's, like, some distant uncle or something. Uncle Fred! Wait till I tell everyone we're related to—"

Grandma tapped her on the head. "Don't go making things up, Casey."

Casey rubbed her head, sighing. Then she caught sight of something else in the book. She drew out an old piece of lined notebook paper and unfolded it. "Hey! This has Mama's name on it. But how come she's writing so sloppy?"

Grandma smiled. "It was her first spelling test. She was only seven years old!"

"Get out of here," Casey said. "My mother was never seven years old."

Jamal and Grandma CeCe burst out laughing.

"Look." Casey pointed to the bottom of the page. "She spelled 'milk' wrong." She laughed, then grew quiet. "It makes me miss her," she said softly.

Grandma CeCe pulled Casey to her. "You'll see her again soon, honey bee."

"I know," Casey said. "I just wish she were here."

"She *is* here," Jamal said quickly, not wanting to see

Casey cry. "She's right there." He pointed at the spelling test.

Casey smiled again. "You're right." She looked at Grandma. "The reunion starts in two hours. Can we put the book out for people to look at?" she asked.

Grandma looked at her watch. "Two hours? Oh, lord!" She jumped to her feet. "We've got to get a move on!"

"The book, Grandma," Casey persisted.

Grandma took the spelling test from Casey, folded it, and pressed it back in the book. Then she closed the book and looked from Casey to Jamal. "I don't know. It's so fragile."

"We'll tell people to be careful," Jamal promised.

"Okay," Grandma said finally, handing the book to Jamal. "I have too many things to do to argue about it. I'm putting you two in charge. Don't have a lot of people opening it. That book is too old to be messed with."

"We won't," Jamal said, following behind her.

"We'll guard it like hawks," Casey added.

Grandma still looked nervous.

"Don't worry, Grandma," Jamal said confidently. "It's just family. What could possibly happen?"

Chapter 2

"Smells good in here," Jamal said, coming into the kitchen with the book. His sister Danitra was at the stove. Danitra was almost as good a cook as Grandma CeCe, in Jamal's opinion. Danitra's specialty was all kinds of African food.

"Check this out, Jamal," Casey said, beckoning Jamal over to the table, where she sat poring over the guest list. "Cory *and* Michelle are coming. Two brats in the same house." She wrinkled her nose.

"Takes one to know one," Jamal said, sitting down across from her. He smiled to show her he was kidding.

"Maybe they're not such brats anymore," Danitra said. She added more water to a huge silver-colored boiler that sat bubbling on the stove. "You haven't seen them for years."

Casey shook her head. "Once a brat, always a brat—that's all she wrote!"

Danitra laughed, winking at Casey. They were dressed almost identically—baggy red shorts and striped T-shirts. Danitra had even braided Casey's hair into tiny ropes that hung down to her shoulders. Casey was hoping people would think the braids were dreads. Her mother had said she couldn't start growing real dreads, like the kind they wore in Digable Planets, until she was eighteen.

"Who else is on that list?" Jamal asked, pulling the page across the table.

"Everybody who's anybody," Casey told him. "Plus Aunt Estelle. You look at the list, I'll look at the book."

Grandma CeCe bustled in and checked under the lid of a huge black pot. "This smells good, Danitra. But go easy on the spices. Estelle will have a fit if she eats something she thinks is overseasoned.

"You kids take that book out to the table with the rest of the family mementos," she added, looking at Casey. "Casey, why don't you give Aunt Estelle a call and make sure she doesn't mind it being out."

"Ugh. Do I have to?" Casey groaned. "She's such a mean old—"

"Casey!" Grandma exclaimed, trying not to laugh.

Grumbling, Casey made her way slowly out of the kitchen to the phone in the living room. There was a tiny book sitting by the telephone with phone numbers in it. She looked up Estelle, but there was nothing listed under E.

After a moment Casey shook her head. "Real bright, Casey," she said to herself. Of course Aunt Estelle wouldn't be listed under E. The book was alphabetized by last names, and her last name was Harmon! Casey turned to the Hs.

After about a hundred rings a crackly old voice answered. When Casey asked her about the book, Aunt Estelle had to think for a moment before she remembered. When she finally agreed that it was all right to display the book, Casey felt herself relax.

"Thanks, Aunt Estelle," she said, really meaning it.

"Thanks, nothing. If anything happens to that book, I'm holding the Jenkins household responsible. As a matter of fact, I've got a mind to take it right back home with me—make sure it's safe. . . . "

Casey wasn't really listening any more. The doorbell rang. She said goodbye quickly, then ran to answer it.

"Hey!" Alex Fernandez greeted her. He stood there with Hector Carrero. "Guess who's coming to dinner?"

"Hey yourself," Casey said. "Not you." She started to close the door, then swung it open again. "Psych."

Alex rolled his eyes. "You remember Hector?"

"What do you think I have, amnesia?"

Hector laughed. "Here," he said, handing Casey a pink rubber handball. "You have to sign it."

"Why?" Casey asked.

"Because that's what everybody does—signs everybody else's handballs."

She snorted and handed the ball back to him. "Wrong. I'm not everybody."

"Hey, guys," Jamal said from behind Casey. He looked down at her. "Well, aren't you going to let them in?"

Casey stepped back, and Alex and Hector walked into the living room. "Jamal, why did you sweet-talk Grandma CeCe into inviting these guys to the reunion? They're just here to be nosy and eat all our food," she said.

Alex raised one eyebrow and smiled. "You mean you left some for us?"

Casey grinned back. She really liked Alex and Hector. She was always glad to see them. "Where's Gaby?" she asked.

"On her way," Alex promised. "You know *she* won't miss a chance to be nosy."

In the living room, Danitra had thrown African kinte cloth prints over the back of the sofa. Earlier, Casey had vacuumed the hardwood floor and dusted. Now the room looked neat and welcoming. Grandma had thrown a piece of fabric over the television and set a bowl of nuts on top of it so no one would think of turning it on during the reunion.

"We have the coolest thing," Casey said. "We can't show you until the whole team's here. But when everybody gets here, you'll see what separates us from everybody else and makes us the absolute best family in the whole world!"

"Give me a break," Hector said. But Casey saw his eyes lighting up with curiosity.

"Ha, ha. You want to know, but you have to wait," she sang, doing a small dance around him.

The doorbell rang again. This time it was Gaby, Alex's younger sister. "Hey, Casey," she said. Her brown eyes were shining. "Guess what? I broke a board today in karate." She slammed her hand into the air. "Keeyaaaiii! Just like that! It cracked in two."

Casey grinned. "Now if Alex gives you a problem, you can crack *him* in two."

Gaby nodded, pulling her dark hair back into a ponytail. "Ever since he started being a 'big brother' to Hector, he thinks he's everybody's big brother! Hector comes over and Alex acts like he's somebody's dad."

Casey nodded, but she didn't say anything. Hector's dad wasn't in the picture. He lived alone with his mother. Casey knew that could be hard—her own parents were divorced. Hector probably didn't mind if Alex acted like a dad sometimes.

Lenni Frazier and Tina Nguyen came in from the kitchen just then. "We followed our noses," Tina said.

"Yeah," Lenni agreed. "They led us to the kitchen door." She held up a chicken wing and took a bite. "Mmmm!"

Everyone gathered around the table in the dining area. All the family keepsakes were displayed there. Next to the trumpet, in the place of honor, was the old book.

Hector let out a low whistle. "*Mira,* Alex! That book must be a thousand years old!"

"Well, at least a hundred," Alex said. He touched the cover with his fingertips. "It must be worth something. I read that old books in good condition can sell for lots of money."

Gaby circled the table, checking the book out from all angles. "You should put it under glass with a lock, like they do in museums. What if something happens to it?"

"Oh, brother," Alex said, rolling his eyes. "Nobody's going to take it. It's a family reunion."

Gaby stuck out her tongue at him. "Like I don't know that!"

"Our Aunt Estelle gave it to Grandma CeCe a long time ago. It's full of old letters and stuff about our family," Casey explained. "Grandma's afraid to let people look through it 'cause it's so fragile. We saw a little bit of what's inside, but I'm dying to have a good long look!"

Just then, the book began to glow.

"Look!" Hector said. "Ghostwriter!"

The team gathered around. Casey uncapped the black pen that hung from a string around her neck. Every member of the team had one. That way they were always ready to write to Ghostwriter—and to each other.

WELCOME TO OUR FAMILY REUNION, GHOSTWRITER! Casey wrote on a scrap of paper from her pocket. THE TEAM'S ALL HERE, READY TO KICK BACK AND PIG OUT. DANITRA AND GRANDMA ARE COOKING UP A STORM!

Ghostwriter's glow swept over the words. A moment later he picked up some of the letters from Casey's note. A new message hung glowing in the air:

STAY CLOSE. KEEP WATCH!

Chapter 3

"Huh?" Casey said.

"What do you think Ghostwriter is trying to tell us?" Lenni asked Jamal.

Jamal stared at the message, then at the old book. Ghostwriter was making it glow again. "I don't know," he said slowly. "But it sounds big. Let's ask."

He was uncapping his own pen when Grandma CeCe hurried in. "If you all stare at that old book any more you'll wear the words right off the pages," she scolded. "I put out a plate of chicken in the kitchen. You little people get busy on that and stay out of here, all right?"

Jamal frowned. "Some of us aren't so little anymore, Grandma," he called. "Some of us are in high school!"

"Oh, excuse me, Mr. Man," Grandma said with a smile. Casey and Gaby snickered.

Grandma followed the team into the kitchen. Danitra

was still at the stove, and Mr. Jenkins was standing at the counter unloading bags of groceries. Casey felt frustrated. They couldn't write to Ghostwriter with all these adults around! Their questions would have to wait.

Tina munched on a drumstick. "You have lots of great old stuff," she told Grandma CeCe.

Grandma smiled as she poured lemonade into glasses. "Everything out there has been in this family for years," she said. "For a long time before Luther and I bought this house." She shook her head. "If memories could talk . . ."

"Speaking of talking," she added to Casey and Jamal, "Estelle called back a minute ago. She says she wants the *Narrative of the Life of Frederick Douglass* back after the reunion."

Casey swallowed a bite of chicken. "That's not fair!" she complained. "It's been here forever and ever. It should stay here. And Aunt Estelle lives all the way up in Harlem. We'll never get to look at the book!"

"Well, Estelle and I will talk," Grandma said, pulling one of Casey's braids. "Maybe I can get her to change her mind. The woman *is* a little crabby, but she's reasonable."

A few minutes later Jamal and Danitra's mother came in, wearing an African print dress and headband. "I see our first guests are here," she said with a smile.

"You look beautiful," Gaby said. She showed Mrs. Jenkins the patch on her jeans. It was made out of a fabric like Mrs. Jenkins's dress.

"See, Mama, I told you you'd look great in kinte cloth," Danitra chimed in.

"Yes, you did," Mrs. Jenkins admitted. "Thank you, Danitra." She turned to Jamal. "How about if you head up the decorations team, sugar pie?"

Jamal sighed and stood up. "Okay, team, let's see what we can do to help this woman," he said.

In the living room, Mrs. Jenkins handed Jamal some rolls of red, gold, and green crepe paper. "Hang this across the living room. And someone be in charge of answering the door. I'm going upstairs to do some last-minute cleaning."

She winked, then headed up the stairs. As soon as she was out of sight Hector headed for the memento table. "I want to see if the book is still glow—hey! Jamal!"

"Don't yell, I can hear," Jamal said. "What's up?"

"Did you—um—do some rearranging while we weren't looking?"

"Of course not," Jamal said. He tacked the crepe across the wall behind the couch with tape. Alex held the other end.

"Then somebody is not being funny around here." Hector ran his hand across an empty space on the coffee table.

Tina stopped arranging plastic knives and forks on the dinner table and came over. Lenni followed her.

Lenni gasped. "Gone," she said. "The book is gone!"

Chapter 4

"Grandma CeCe will skin us alive!" Jamal said. "It has to be here somewhere."

Lenni kneeled down to look under the couch. "It couldn't have just vanished."

Gaby opened the closet and pushed some itchy-looking winter coats aside. There were lots of pairs of galoshes and two beat-up tennis rackets leaning against the wall, but not much else. She turned to Tina. "Could someone have sneaked in while we were eating?"

Tina shook her head. "It's daylight. People don't rob houses in daylight. Do they?"

Gaby frowned.

Hector came in from outside. His face was twisted into a worried frown. "I checked under the bushes and around the yard," he reported. "Nothing."

"Maybe Grandma took it for some reason," Jamal said. "Casey, did you notice her picking it up? Casey?"

He looked around, noticing for the first time that Casey wasn't in the living room with the rest of the team.

"I'm beginning to get an idea," he said. He headed for the stairs. On the way, he noticed the basement door was half open. He remembered closing it after he, Grandma, and Casey had left the basement earlier.

He pulled it all the way open. There was a dim light coming up from the bottom of the stairs. "I think the search is over," he said to the team. Then he stuck his head down the stairs and yelled, *"Casey!"*

Casey's face appeared in the gloom, looking guiltily up at Jamal. "All right, already," she said. "I just wanted a real good look inside." Her eyes lit up. "Jamal—you have to see this!"

"You had us scared to death," Jamal told her. He flipped the light switch and made his way carefully down the basement stairs. When he reached Casey, he let out a sigh of relief. The book was safe and sound in her lap.

"Ghostwriter's been reading with me," Casey said proudly. "He seems very interested in Frederick Douglass. Here, look at these pictures!"

Casey turned to the back of the book. There were about a dozen photos crammed inside the dust jacket. The people in them looked faded and old, dressed in clothes from what seemed like centuries ago.

Jamal stared at the photos, forgetting he was mad at Casey. "Those must be relatives," he said.

"I just wanted to see this," Casey explained. "If Aunt Estelle takes the book, we might not ever see any of this stuff. Look, here's a baby picture of your dad."

Jamal looked closely at the smiling little boy. It was his father, all right. Jamal recognized the eyes.

"And look at these flowers," Casey said. "Somebody must have been in love."

Jamal carefully turned the pages. A neat stack of letters tied with pale, fragile-looking string was stuck between chapter eleven and chapter twelve. A birth certificate, with a name neither of them could make out, lay between the next two pages.

Jamal got a funny feeling in his stomach as he looked at the book. One day, he and Casey would be a part of it, too. Pictures of them, letters they had written from camp, and report cards would be added to the book. Maybe, years from now, two other kids would look through it and wonder about Frederick Douglass and all the other people between its pages.

"Jamal! Casey! Upstairs *now*!" Grandma CeCe's voice was exasperated.

Casey closed the book quickly and followed her cousin up to the living room. She was surprised to see that people had already started to arrive.

"I told you two to leave the book alone," Grandma CeCe whispered, taking the book and replacing it on the table. "Now go say hello to your relatives. And keep an eye out for that delivery boy from Simon's Deli. The cold cuts were supposed to be delivered two hours ago. Last time I use Simon's for a special occasion."

"Don't worry," Casey said. "There's enough groundnut stew and milk pudding that no one will want any cold cuts."

"Estelle won't eat any of that African stuff, not if I know her," Grandma fretted. "Too much flavor in it."

"There's my baby," an ancient voice cracked. Casey smothered a groan. Aunt Estelle!

She was dressed in a pale blue pantsuit that perfectly matched her blue hat. A pair of frameless glasses hung from a silver chain around her neck. She walked over to the table, and Casey cringed. She remembered Aunt Estelle's big, sloppy kisses.

But Aunt Estelle sailed right past Casey, laying a gnarled hand on the book. "I've missed it," she croaked. When she smiled, one gold tooth flashed. The smile disappeared as quickly as it had come.

"Do you know who Frederick Douglass was?" she asked

Casey. Before Casey could answer, Aunt Estelle shook her head. Her eyes were focused on a place right above Casey's head. "Didn't think you did. Kids today are so ignorant. Hardly even know how to read and write!"

"I can read and write," Casey said indignantly. "I have a friend I can only talk to in writing—"

She broke off as she felt a sharp kick on the back of her leg. "Shhh!" Gaby hissed. "You can't tell her about you know who!"

Casey was horrified. She had nearly spilled the beans about Ghostwriter! But when she looked back at Aunt Estelle she felt better. It was obvious Aunt Estelle hadn't been listening. She was still going on about Frederick Douglass.

"Got another book on this man right in my house. It isn't as good as the autobiography, of course, but it'll tell you what you need to know." Her gnarled fingers closed on Casey's shoulder. "You come up to my place and I'll lend it to you."

"Uh—sure," Casey mumbled. She looked around for an escape.

Just then Grandma CeCe came up with Jamal. Jamal looked as if someone had just pinched his ear.

"I see you've already found my youngest granddaughter," Grandma said to Aunt Estelle.

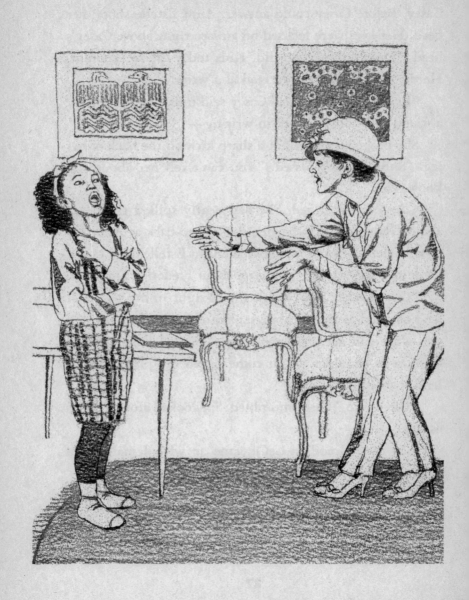

"Well, I haven't gotten a proper hello yet," Aunt Estelle complained. "Come a little closer, girl."

The next thing Casey knew, Grandma was pushing her forward and Aunt Estelle was placing a big wet one right smack-dab in the middle of her forehead.

"Your turn," Casey whispered as she passed Jamal, trying to wipe her forehead in a way that Aunt Estelle wouldn't notice.

A group had begun forming around the food Grandma CeCe and Danitra had put out. At the kitchen door, Mr. and Mrs. Jenkins stood laughing with some people Casey didn't recognize. Across the room, Gaby smiled at her, holding up a glass of punch.

When the doorbell rang, Casey and Jamal both grabbed the chance to answer it and escape from Aunt Estelle. A delivery boy stood on the front steps, a huge platter of plastic-covered cold cuts in his hands. He was tall and curly-haired, wearing a red shirt with "AL" embroidered across the right pocket. "I've seen you playing basketball in the park on Saturdays," Jamal said to him.

The boy nodded. "Where does this go?" he asked, holding the platter out.

"Over here." Jamal cleared a space in the crowd so the boy could get through. "Any roasted turkey on there?"

The boy nodded again. "You got your ham, your roasted turkey, your three kinds of cheeses, two kinds of pickles, horseradish, and mustard. Simon's doesn't play around when putting a platter down."

Casey and Jamal laughed.

"Hey, cool," the boy said, eyeing the trumpet on the memento table. "You play?"

Jamal shook his head. "It belonged to my great-grandfather. Maybe I'll take lessons."

Casey covered her hands with her ears. "Wait until I go back to Detroit!"

"Whoa!" the delivery boy exclaimed, reaching out a hand to the Frederick Douglass book. "Is this Freddy D?"

Casey frowned. "No. It's Frederick Douglass—and a whole bunch of other people, too," she said.

The boy touched the book tenderly. "I just finished taking a course on him up at City College. You know my homeboy was dyslexic?"

"Dis who?"

The boy smiled. "He couldn't read or write without a whole lot of trouble. But look at all the stuff he did— founded a newspaper, wrote a bunch of books, *and* worked to free the slaves," he said. Then he pointed at the book. "That looks old—like a first edition. My class would flip if they saw it." He sighed. "What I wouldn't give for a first edition of the *Narrative of the Life of Frederick Douglass*."

Casey felt uncomfortable. "Yeah, well," she mumbled.

"Hey, I have to go," the delivery boy said, checking his watch. "You enjoy those cold cuts. I'll be back later to pick up the platter." He cast one last glance at the old book, then turned and left.

Chapter 5

"Casey! Jamal! Come on over here and say hello to your uncle Albert," Mr. Jenkins called.

Casey and Jamal picked their way across the crowded room. A tall, thin man with silver-gray hair and wrinkling skin smiled at them. "Who are these big, fine people?" he said, limping toward them with the help of a cane. "Are they any relation to me?"

Casey laughed and hugged him. "You know us, Uncle Albert," she said.

"Maybe I do, maybe I don't," Uncle Albert said, a glint in his eye.

Casey had met Uncle Albert a year ago when she came to New York for the man's sixty-fifth birthday. She had liked him immediately. It was too bad the Jenkins family didn't see him very often. He walked with a cane because of an old war injury. That made it hard for him to get all the way to Brooklyn from Harlem, where he lived.

"You remember my daughter, Renee," Uncle Albert was saying. He had his arm around a tall woman. Her hair was in dreads wrapped up in a scarf. Jamal and Casey shook her hand.

"Hi, guys," Renee said with a smile. "This is my fiancé, Milton." She put her hand on the arm of a man in wire-rimmed glasses. He had light-brown skin and close-cropped hair, and he was wearing what looked like a very expensive suit.

"Milton made the most romantic proposal in *history*," Renee was saying to Mr. Jenkins. "You should have seen it, Cousin Reggie. Not a single spoken word." She beamed at Milton. "Right, honey?"

Jamal and Casey exchanged looks. "Oh, brother," Casey whispered.

Renee pointed at the tray of cold cuts nearby. "See, Milton, they have cold cuts. You can make yourself that ham, horseradish, and pickle club sandwich you love so much. Didn't I tell you there'd be plenty of stuff to eat? Aunt CeCe doesn't play when it comes to food. We won't need to eat for days after this. When we go on our country picnic tomorrow, we won't even have to pack any food."

"Milton's studying to be an entertainment lawyer," Uncle Albert was saying to Jamal's father.

Milton spoke for the first time as he layered ham, horse-

radish, and pickles on a piece of rye bread. "Yes, I get to meet all sorts of interesting people. Just last week I had coffee with a man who claims he's a long-lost brother of Tina Turner. He's writing a book about it."

"Really," Mr. Jenkins said politely. "I guess there's a lot of money in the entertainment industry, eh?"

Renee laughed. "One day, we hope. Right now Milton's still a poor student."

"Even if he doesn't like to live like one, with his tailored suits and his book collecting," Uncle Albert added.

"We have a book that we think might be valuable," Jamal told Milton. "Want to see it?"

"Sure," Milton said with a smile.

Casey tagged along as Milton and Jamal went over to the memento table. "It's by Frederick Douglass," Jamal explained to Milton.

"You know he was dyslexic," Casey chimed in.

Jamal shook his head. "Parrot."

"Am not!" Casey protested.

Milton picked up the book casually. Then he looked at it more closely. "Wow!" he said. "A book like this could get you a couple of thousand dollars, easily. I know a guy who'd offer cash for it." He turned it over to look at the back cover.

"Really?" Casey asked in excitement.

"Well, it's not for sale!" an angry voice said. Casey and Jamal turned to see Aunt Estelle struggling toward them through the crowd.

"She must have been an ear in another life," Casey whispered.

"How are you, Miss Harmon?" Milton asked with a polite smile.

"Been better," Aunt Estelle snapped. "That book is going back to my house and staying there." Without waiting for anyone to answer her, she moved on toward Uncle Albert. "I've got a few words for you, mister, about not ever picking up the telephone to give me a call . . ." Casey heard her say. Then she was gone.

It was after eight o'clock when the last guest finally went home. Everyone was exhausted, but the team had volunteered to help clean up. Mr. and Mrs. Jenkins were more than grateful for the offer.

"Your family throws some pretty fun parties," Hector said over his shoulder. He was removing the last of the crepe paper from the walls.

"We talked to your aunt Estelle for a long time," Lenni remarked.

"Yeah. She seems really sweet," Gaby added.

"*Aunt Estelle?*" Casey and Jamal said together.

"Maybe you were talking to someone else with the same name." Casey laughed. "Our Aunt Estelle is *not* sweet."

Tina dragged a huge garbage bag from the kitchen and began stuffing paper plates into it.

"Yes she is," Gaby said. "She invited us to come visit her in Harlem. She said 'come anytime.'"

She and Lenni dragged a full bag of garbage outside. Through the front door, Casey saw that it was almost dark out. Up and down the block, people sat on their stoops chatting in the warm summer night.

"How about the table with all the family mementos?" Tina asked. "Should we clean that up?"

"Grandma CeCe said she'll put that stuff away in the morning," Jamal said. He glanced at the table. Then he did a double take. "Wait a minute! Casey!"

"What?" Casey demanded. She didn't like Jamal's tone of voice.

"You wouldn't by any chance have made off with the Frederick Douglass book again?"

Casey folded her arms across her chest. "Of course not," she retorted. Then she understood what Jamal was saying. She looked with alarm at the table. The spot where the book had been was empty again.

"You know what happened to it. Old Estelle took it after all," she said.

Jamal sighed. "Yeah, I guess that must be it. That's that, huh?"

"That's what?" Lenni asked, closing the front door behind Gaby.

Jamal explained that Aunt Estelle had taken the Frederick Douglass book home with her. Lenni frowned and looked at Gaby.

"I thought she said she was going to let it stay here after all," Lenni said.

Gaby nodded. "She did. Grandma Jenkins came up and talked to her for a few minutes. After that she said, 'CeCe can keep that old book if it means that much to her.' That was right before she invited us to come visit her."

"Wait a minute," Casey said, raising her hands. "Are you sure?"

Gaby and Lenni nodded together.

"Uh-oh," Alex said. The whole team stared at the spot on the table where the book had been.

"I've got a creepy feeling," Casey said. "If Aunt Estelle didn't take it . . ."

Jamal finished Casey's sentence. "Then . . . who did?"

Chapter 6

"I'll go ask Grandma if she knows anything," Jamal said, heading for the stairs.

"Don't get her all worried," Casey said. "It could be the book is safe somewhere."

Jamal nodded. "I know how to handle it."

A few minutes later he hurried back down the stairs. "She doesn't know anything about it," he reported. "She says we should ask Aunt Estelle about it in the morning."

Tina was sitting on the couch next to Hector. She pulled a black-and-white notebook out of her bag. "Just in case," she said. "Casebook." Opening the notebook, she turned to a blank page and wrote "SUSPECTS" at the top.

"Aunt Estelle," Casey said immediately. "And under 'EVIDENCE,' write down that she's a mean old thing."

"Casey, that isn't evidence," Jamal said. "That's just what you think."

"But even if she took the book, can we really say she's a suspect?" Tina said. "I mean, after all, it's her book."

"Tina's right," Alex said.

Casey scowled. "I say put her on the list," she insisted.

Tina shrugged and wrote it down. "Okay. Who else?"

Jamal thought for a moment. "Hey! That guy who delivered the deli food was really into it," he said.

"That's good," Lenni said excitedly. "Do we have any evidence?"

"Well, he said he'd give anything for a first edition of the *Narrative of the Life of Frederick Douglass*," Jamal said.

"But he left before the book disappeared," Gaby objected.

"No! No! He came back!" Hector practically yelled. He was so excited he jumped up out of his seat. "I let him in. It was around eight o'clock. He had to pick up the platter. I bet he took the book then. Yeah!" He pounded his fist on the arm of the couch. "Call the police! We have to stop him. He might have sold that book for millions of dollars already!"

Tina was scribbling frantically. "Calm down, Hector," she said. "It's too late for him to sell the book tonight. If he did take it, we can probably catch him tomorrow."

"But first we have to get real proof," Jamal added.

"Let's ask Ghostwriter!" Gaby said. "He could find the book and read what's around it."

"Good idea," Lenni said, nodding. "Maybe he can clear up this whole mystery for us."

Tina quickly wrote a note to Ghostwriter, explaining what had happened. CAN YOU HELP US FIND THE BOOK? she finished.

Ghostwriter grabbed letters off the page and threw them up into the air. His message read:

CALAMITY! HISTORY COULD BE LOST!

"Ghostwriter's really upset," Gaby exclaimed. She uncapped her own pen. DON'T WORRY, GW, she wrote. WE'LL FIND IT.

Ghostwriter zipped off on his mission. "What other suspects do we have?" Alex said.

"What about my cousin Renee's fiancé, Milton?" Casey said. "He kind of gave me the creeps."

"You can't put someone on the list because they give you the creeps," Alex said. "If we all did that, we'd have so many suspects we wouldn't know where to start."

"But Milton is a book collector," Jamal pointed out.

"Yeah, and he said he knew people who would pay *cash* for the Frederick Douglass book," Casey added. She stuck her tongue out at Alex.

"Well, that sounds more like real evidence," Alex admitted. "Let's add him to the list."

As Tina wrote in the casebook, Ghostwriter appeared again. The letters on the page started scrambling.

"Come look, everybody," Tina said.

The team gathered eagerly around the casebook.

54TH REGIMENT, Ghostwriter wrote.

"What does that mean?" Lenni asked.

"What's 'regiment'?" Casey added.

Jamal went over to the bookshelf and pulled down a huge dictionary. Casey peered over his shoulder as he flipped to the Rs. "There it is," he said. Casey read aloud from the page:

reg i ment—n. 1. *Military. A unit of ground forces. —*
v. 2. To manage in a strict manner.

" 'A strict manner' smells like Aunt Estelle to me," Casey whispered. Jamal rolled his eyes.

"How do we know which definition is the right one?" Hector asked. He looked worried.

"Well, think about the way 'regiment' is used," Alex told him. " '54th Regiment'—that's a *thing*, not an action. It's got to be the first definition."

"So the 54th Regiment is the fifty-fourth unit of ground forces," Lenni said. She wrinkled her nose. "I still don't get what it has to do with the book."

GW, Jamal wrote. CAN YOU FIND ANYTHING ELSE AROUND THE BOOK THAT MIGHT HELP US? LIKE A NAME?

I'LL LOOK, Ghostwriter promised, and zipped away.

"54th Regiment. Sounds like it has something to do with war," Alex said.

"War!" Casey exclaimed. "Like the one where Uncle Albert got his leg wounded. Maybe Ghostwriter was reading from the book! Maybe it has something in it about Uncle Albert fighting. Maybe it tells how he got hurt."

"Or maybe," Hector said, "the book is in your uncle Albert's house."

There was silence. Jamal and Casey looked at each other.

"Uncle Albert wouldn't take the book," Jamal said after a moment. "He's not like that."

"Are you sure?" Lenni asked quietly.

Jamal scowled and looked down. "I guess we can't rule him out," he muttered.

Casey took her own pen from around her neck and reluctantly added Uncle Albert's name to the casebook. Under "EVIDENCE," she wrote "54TH REGIMENT—WAR?"

Just then Ghostwriter came back. He started scrambling letters around on the open pages of the dictionary.

YR LOVG ALBT

"What the—" Hector said.

"Don't panic, Hector," Lenni told him. "Those words are probably contractions. In contractions, you shorten the words by taking some letters out."

"All we have to do is add the letters back in again," Gaby chimed in.

Lenni took the casebook from Casey and began writing.

"Yr . . . yer . . . your!" she muttered. "The first word could be 'your.' "

"*Lo entiendo*—I get it!" Hector said. "Cool!"

"Lovg," Jamal said. "Loveg. Lovig. Loving?"

"Sounds good!" Gaby said excitedly. "What about Albt?"

"Alebt," Hector said. "Your loving Alebt." He looked around at the other team members. "Who's Alebt?"

Jamal put his finger to his lips and stared at the four letters. "Alebt . . . Albet . . . Albets . . . Albert! Your loving Albert!" He looked excited—but only for a second. Then his smile faded. "*Uncle* Albert," he added.

"Uh-oh," Casey said. "This book might be a lot easier to find than we thought."

Chapter 7

At nine-thirty the next morning, Casey nervously dialed Aunt Estelle's number. She didn't know what answer she hoped to get. If Aunt Estelle *had* taken the book home with her, then it wouldn't belong to Casey and Jamal any more. But if Aunt Estelle *hadn't* taken the book, then that meant someone else had . . . maybe even someone nice, like Uncle Albert.

Aunt Estelle answered after the third ring. "Hi, it's Casey," Casey began. "I was wondering—"

"Wasn't that some party?" Aunt Estelle said cheerfully. "I could have danced all night!"

Casey nearly choked. Aunt Estelle, dancing? "Uh—really?" she said.

"Ask her about the book!" Jamal whispered, poking her.

Casey frowned at him. "Yeah, the party was fun," she agreed with Aunt Estelle. "But I was wondering—"

"If I had a good time? Well, sure I did, child. The family ought to get together more often. Say, when are you and your cousin Jamal coming up to see me?"

"Soon, really soon," Casey said. She rushed on nervously. "In fact, we were wondering if you have the Frederick Douglass book——"

"Sure, sure! I didn't think you were listening," Aunt Estelle said. "Well, isn't that nice. Come on up here and get it. And bring your friends! I'll make you kids something to eat."

Casey's heart raced. "You mean . . . we can have it?"

"Of course," said Aunt Estelle. "If you want it, it's yours. I've already read the thing."

Casey said goodbye and hung up. "She's a fast reader," she told Jamal. Then she did a little dance of joy. "She has the book! It wasn't stolen! She said we could go get it!"

Jamal called the rest of the team to let them know they had found the book. They all agreed to meet at the subway station in half an hour and go uptown together.

They took the A train to 125th Street, one of the main shopping streets in Harlem. The neighborhood was alive. Vendors were crowded along the sidewalk, selling T-shirts, jewelry, and hats from folding tables. Others had laid out beautiful African carvings on blankets. Lenni and Gaby stopped at a table to look at some cowrie-shell necklaces.

"Come on," Jamal urged. "We don't have all day!"

Farther down the block they passed a man selling incense and perfume oils. Lenni stopped and quickly put some oil on her wrists, but she didn't buy anything.

"Lenni! We have to get there before Aunt Estelle changes her mind," Casey said impatiently.

Soon they were ringing the bell at Aunt Estelle's building. When she buzzed them in, they trooped up the stairs to her second-floor apartment.

She seemed overjoyed to see the team. She had set out a plate of sandwiches and a pitcher of fruit punch. Her small apartment was bright and clean. It was filled with ancient pictures of people Casey didn't recognize.

"Who's that?" Casey asked, pointing to a picture of a pretty little girl with her hair in two braids. She seemed distant and a bit sad in the picture. She stared at the camera as if she didn't know what she was supposed to do in front of it. The picture was old. Its yellow edges curled behind the wooden frame.

"That's me," Aunt Estelle said with a smile. "I must have been about your age."

Casey gasped. She'd never thought of Aunt Estelle as being anything but old! She looked at the picture more closely. The girl looked like someone she would have been friends with.

"I'm glad you want to learn more about Frederick Douglass," Aunt Estelle said. "You know, he was a man who understood the importance of history. He wrote three accounts of his own life—the life of a black slave. He knew if he didn't, people might not ever learn the truth about those terrible times. See, there wasn't anybody writing much about black folks' history, about black folks' lives, back then. Not anybody who knew what it was really like." She paused for a moment. Her eyes had a faraway look, like the eyes of the little girl in the picture. "That's why I started to store all those family keepsakes in the book he wrote," she finished. "Those things tell the history of our black family. It just seemed the most fitting thing to do."

Casey nodded. What Aunt Estelle was saying made a lot of sense. She decided that as soon as the *Narrative of the Life of Frederick Douglass* was back in her hands, she would read it cover to cover.

Hector wandered over to a shelf full of photos. "Who's this?" he asked, pointing to a picture of a baby swaddled in pale blankets. The baby was bald and toothless. Still, it grinned into the camera.

Jamal leaned over to get a better look at the picture. "That's one ugly baby," he said.

Aunt Estelle laughed. "I'll just have to tell CeCe you said that about her."

"That's Grandma?" Jamal gasped. His mouth fell open.

"None other," Aunt Estelle said. "Baddest child there ever was. Still stubborn as a mule, to this very day." She sat down in an overstuffed chair beside the window. "Bring your plates on over here and get comfortable, kids," she said.

"What was so bad about Grandma CeCe?" Gaby asked, sitting on a small stool near Aunt Estelle's feet.

"Oh, everything," Aunt Estelle said, waving her hand. "She used to go up to this creek back behind the farm my mama owned, and she would lie on her back in the water looking like she drowned. First time I saw her I started crying so hard I couldn't help myself. Imagine me, a grown woman already, and here is this little girl making me cry. Then all of a sudden she popped up and yelled 'Gotcha!' like it was the funniest thing in the world."

"You know what?" Jamal said, smiling. "That sounds like Casey."

Everyone laughed.

"We had some good old days," Aunt Estelle said. She sighed. "Now look at us, two old ladies."

Casey stared at Aunt Estelle. She wasn't acting much like the mean old lady Casey remembered. This Aunt Estelle was nice. This Aunt Estelle was even fun!

"How come you don't have a husband?" Casey blurted out. Then she covered her mouth with her hand.

"Casey," Jamal said.

"Sorry," Casey mumbled.

"No, no," Aunt Estelle said. "Ask away. That's how you learn, isn't it? No harm in asking a few questions."

"Then how come?" Casey said quickly.

"Never wanted one," Aunt Estelle replied with a shrug. "Men are too much trouble."

The girls all giggled. "Hear that, Alex? You are too much trouble," Gaby said.

"Hey!" Alex protested.

Aunt Estelle leaned forward and pulled back the curtain beside her chair. "Looks hot outside."

"Tell us more about Grandma CeCe and you," Casey said eagerly. She leaned forward against Aunt Estelle's leg. It was bony and warm.

Aunt Estelle leaned back in her chair again. "Hmmph. Let me see," she said. "Well, I used to baby-sit her, you know. She couldn't have been more than four or five when this happened. . . ."

The team spent the rest of the afternoon listening to Aunt Estelle's stories and eating sandwiches. When Jamal finally looked at the clock, he was surprised to see that it was after four.

He stood up. "We'd better get going," he said.

"So soon?" Aunt Estelle said. She looked sad all of a sudden. She seemed to shrink back a little into herself. Casey suddenly realized she must be lonely, living by herself all the way uptown.

"We'll come again soon, Aunt Estelle," she promised, hugging the elderly woman. "It was fun!"

Aunt Estelle's face lit up. "Well, that's fine. Oh, let me get you the book you came for." She made her way slowly down the hall. Casey gave the team a triumphant smile.

A few minutes later Aunt Estelle came back into the living room. She was carrying a thin paperback book.

Casey groaned. "That's not Frederick Douglass's autobiography."

"It's not as good as the autobiography," Aunt Estelle said, nodding. "But you can still learn from it."

"We wanted the one that was on the table at the reunion," Casey explained.

Aunt Estelle frowned. "Well, you already have it," she said. "Didn't CeCe tell you? I told her she could keep that book, since it meant so much to everyone. Gives me a reason to get to Brooklyn more, anyhow—I can come down and tell you about all the people hidden between the pages." She patted Casey's shoulder. "Go on home," she said. "That's where I left the book."

. . .

When the team was back in the subway station, Tina opened the casebook again.

"So I guess we have a case after all," she said.

Casey and Jamal nodded gloomily.

"But Aunt Estelle is out of the running," Alex said. He took the pen from around his neck and crossed out Aunt Estelle's name.

Lenni nodded. "After all, she doesn't have any reason to lie about not having the book—it belongs to her."

"So what do we do now?" Gaby asked. She gazed over Tina's shoulder at the casebook.

Tina flipped through the pages. "Well, we still have three suspects: the deli delivery guy, Renee's boyfriend Milton, and Uncle Albert."

"I think we should investigate that deli guy. It has to be him," Casey said quickly. "Or Milton."

Tina shook her head. "Sorry, Casey. But the clues Ghostwriter found make Uncle Albert look pretty suspicious." She pointed to the list of evidence. " '54th Regiment' and 'Yr Lovg Albt'—who else could they be about?"

Suddenly the letters on the page began to move around. In a moment a message from Ghostwriter appeared:

CASEY, WHY ARE YOU SAD?

"We'd better tell Ghostwriter what's happening," Hector said.

GW, Tina wrote, THE BOOK IS DEFINITELY MISSING. AUNT ESTELLE DIDN'T HAVE IT. IT LOOKS AS IF SOMEONE STOLE IT. WE'RE ON OUR WAY HOME NOW. CAN YOU HELP US WITH ANY OTHER CLUES?

The subway train pulled into the station and they all got on. They took seats, and Tina opened the casebook again. A moment later a new message from Ghostwriter appeared.

MON'S DELI

L YOU CAN EAT CHEAP!

UPER CLUB 5.95

P/U

1734 MYRTLE AVE 122 E. 125TH ST.
BROOKLYN, NY NEW YORK, NY

Tina quickly copied it down under "Other Clues."

" 'L you can eat cheap'?" Hector read. "What does that mean?"

"I think some letters must be missing," Jamal said. "The letter L by itself isn't a word."

"Maybe the piece of paper that Ghostwriter read this from is torn," Gaby suggested.

Alex squinted at the strange message. "You know what?" he said suddenly. "It looks like it's from a menu or something. The word 'club' could mean a club sandwich. And look at the top—Mon's Deli. Do you think that could be part of 'Simon's Deli'?"

"Hey, yeah," Jamal said. "It's got to be. Look at this first address at the bottom. That's where we got the cold-cuts platter for the party yesterday." He frowned. "I didn't know Simon's had another store in Harlem."

"The deli guy! The deli guy!" Casey practically shouted. "I told you he was the one!"

All the team members looked at each other. "He's definitely a good suspect," Jamal said after a minute.

"We should definitely investigate him," Lenni agreed. "But . . . " She looked from Casey to Jamal. "We also have to investigate your uncle. There are still a lot of clues that point to him."

Casey looked down at her shoes. "Yeah, yeah," she mumbled.

"Ghostwriter's back," Hector said suddenly. He

pointed to a poster across the subway car from the team. It was an advertisement for foot surgery. Only now the letters were all jumping around into new positions. "It looks like he found something else."

HISPANIOLA   300 NAUT. MI., Ghostwriter wrote. 20 N   64 W.

"Hispaniola," Alex said. "That sounds Spanish—you know, like 'Hispanic' and 'Español.' "

"Which means 'Spanish' in Spanish," Hector added.

"But what does the rest of it mean?" Gaby asked.

There was silence. Then Jamal took his pen and wrote:

GHOSTWRITER, WE'RE CONFUSED.

SO AM I, Ghostwriter replied. The letters shivered, then slowly melted down the page.

"I think Ghostwriter is sad, too," Casey said. "He wants us to find the book."

Jamal clapped his hands together. "Well, the best way to do that is to get to work on solving these clues," he said in a brisk voice. "Let's see. 'Naut. mi.' could be an abbreviation for something."

"A what?" Hector said.

"An abbreviation—like writing oz. for 'ounces' or ft. for 'feet,' " Jamal explained.

Suddenly Gaby snapped her fingers. "Or mi. for 'miles'!" she said. "Maybe it's 300 miles!"

"What about the 'naut.'?" Tina reminded her. "What's that?"

No one had any ideas.

"I think we need to split up," Lenni said after a moment. "Different groups can work on different clues."

"I have to help my parents at the bodega," Alex said. "I promised them I'd be home by five o'clock to sweep and help restock. Papa pays me now for the work I do," he added proudly.

"Okay, the rest of us will work on it," Lenni said. "Tina, can you come to the library with me? Maybe we can figure out what 'Hispaniola' and 'Naut.' mean."

"I'll try to find that delivery kid," Jamal volunteered. "Hector, will you help me?"

"Sure," Hector agreed, looking pleased.

"Gaby and I will talk to Milton," Casey said quickly.

"You can't," Jamal said. "Don't you remember Renee saying that she and Milton were going on a picnic in the country today? They won't be around."

"There's only one thing left for us to do, Casey," said Gaby.

Casey sighed. "Okay. I guess if someone has to talk to

Uncle Albert, I might as well be the one." She stood up as the train groaned to a stop. On the other side of the platform an uptown train was pulling in. "Come on, Gaby. We have to go back to Harlem again. Uncle Albert lives right near Aunt Estelle. We can make that train if we run."

"Meet us at our house at seven," Jamal called.

Gaby and Casey jumped aboard the uptown train just before the doors slid shut. They took seats, and Gaby looked at Casey. "Cheer up," she said. "The book has to be somewhere."

"Yeah," Casey agreed. "I'm just afraid of *where*."

Chapter 8

"Hurry, Tina," Lenni said, racing ahead of her friend. "We don't have much time before the library closes."

The two girls ran down to the end of the block. There Lenni tapped her foot impatiently as they waited for a green light to cross the street. When the light finally changed, they hurried across and up the block to the Brooklyn Public Library. They ran up the steps just as a woman behind the glass door was turning the sign from "open" to "closed."

Lenni groaned and slid into a sitting position. "Now what?"

Tina thought for a second, staring out into the street. All of a sudden, she snapped her fingers.

"Got it," she said. "Let's try the bookstore on Fulton. They have some reference books there."

Lenni was rubbing her ankle. "I think I twisted it," she grumbled. Then suddenly she stopped, staring at her sneaker. There was a sailboat painted on the side, with a big red-and-white sail. Underneath it was written *NAU-TICAL FLYERS*.

"Tina! Look!" Lenni exclaimed. "Nautical! 'Naut.' must stand for 'nautical'! "

"What does it mean?" Tina wanted to know.

Lenni scratched her ear. "I'm not sure. But it must have something to do with sailing. Look at the picture."

Tina took Lenni's hand and pulled her to her feet. "Let's go find some books on sailing," she said.

At the bookstore, a teenaged girl in glasses sat by the cash register, her head bent over a book. She looked up and smiled when Lenni and Tina came in. "Hi. Can I help you?"

"Do you have any books on sailing?" Tina asked.

"Sure. Check in the back, in the sports section," the girl said. "But we're closing in five minutes."

"We'd better work fast," Tina whispered as they made their way past shelves filled with books. "Hmm. Fishing, flying, freestyle Frisbee . . . Frisbee? Is that really a sport?"

Lenni shrugged. "Guess so."

"Sailing!" Tina announced. She pulled a thick book called *Sailing A to Z* down from the shelf and turned to the index. "I'm going to look under 'nautical.' "

Lenni peered over her shoulder. "Look! Nautical miles, page 132," she said excitedly.

Tina quickly flipped to the right page. " 'A nautical

mile is slightly longer than a standard mile,' " she read. " 'In terms of degrees of longitude, it is defined as one second of arc.' "

"Huh?" Lenni said.

"I don't know what it means either," Tina said. "But it doesn't matter. The important thing is, 'naut. mi.' stands for 'nautical miles'—and that's a way of measuring distance when you're sailing."

She opened the casebook and turned to the "Other Clues" page. Under "Hispaniola 300 naut. mi." she wrote down "300 nautical miles."

"So someone is sailing somewhere?" Lenni said.

"Maybe," Tina said doubtfully.

"Closing time," the salesgirl called.

"We'll have to look up 'Hispaniola' later," Tina said. "Come on, let's go over to Jamal's."

"I don't really get any of this," Lenni confessed as they walked.

"Me either," Tina said. "We know we're talking about sailing, but who's on the boat? Where is it going? And why?"

Lenni sighed. "And what does any of it have to do with the stolen book?"

Chapter 9

"Well, hello," Uncle Albert said to Casey and Gaby. He opened his apartment door wide so they could come in. "What a nice surprise!"

The apartment opened into a big, sunny kitchen with a round table in one corner. Casey was surprised to see Renee and Milton seated at the table. She had thought they'd be gone all day on their romantic picnic.

"Let me fix you something cool to drink," Uncle Albert said. He waved the girls to the empty seats at the table. The kitchen smelled of pine-scented cleaner and wood.

"Is lemonade okay?" Uncle Albert asked.

"Great," Gaby said with a smile.

He set two frosty glasses in front of them. "So," he said. "What brings you to old Uncle Albert's house?"

"We—uh—visited Aunt Estelle," Casey said quickly. "And since we were in the neighborhood, we figured we'd drop in on you, too." It wasn't really a fib, she thought. Just sort of.

Uncle Albert smiled. "Well, it's always good to see some young faces around here."

"Yeah," Renee said, clutching Milton's hand. "Especially since I'm going to be an old married lady soon."

"I thought you two were going on a romantic trip today," Casey said.

Milton smiled. "I had some business that came up, so the little lady and I decided to visit her father instead." He gazed fondly at Renee.

Casey glanced at Gaby, who looked like she was trying not to make a face. *Little lady?* Yuck!

"I got called in to work anyway," Renee added. "We have a big deadline at the magazine." She looked at Milton. "We should get going, honey. You have stuff to do before you drop me off, don't you?"

Milton nodded, put his arm across Renee's shoulders, and kissed her on the cheek. Then they both stood up.

"Boy, are you guys mushy," Casey blurted out.

Milton and Renee both laughed as if she'd said something really hilarious. "She's cute," Milton said to Renee. "Listen, I'd like to pick up a sandwich before I do anything else."

"I told you, you could eat anything I have in that fridge," Uncle Albert said. "You said you don't have much money these days. No use wasting it on deli food."

"Don't worry, Pop, the Super Club is only five dollars and ninety-five cents," Milton said. "I can swing it."

Renee grinned. "Milton loves his special sandwiches. Ham, horseradish, and pickle—can you imagine? I don't know where he gets his taste buds from."

Casey took a big gulp of lemonade and eyed Milton. He seemed like a nice enough guy, even if he was so mushy with Renee. He wouldn't have stolen their book, would he? The more she thought about it, the more sure she was that the culprit had to be the deli delivery boy.

"Let me just go phone the deli and order," Milton said. "That way they'll have it ready when I come in to pick it up." He and Renee headed for the living room.

When Gaby and Casey were alone with Uncle Albert, Gaby leaned forward in her chair. "We were wondering if you had seen that autobiography of Frederick Douglass," she said to Uncle Albert.

Casey squirmed in her seat. She'd been putting off the question. But she guessed it was time to get on with it.

"You mean the one that was out yesterday?" Uncle Albert took a long swallow of lemonade, then set his glass down heavily. He frowned. "Last I saw it, it was on the table at your grandma's house, Casey."

"Oh," Casey said. She didn't know what she should ask next. So she stared at Uncle Albert for a long time without blinking. She had seen this on a television show. Whoever blinked first was the guilty one.

Uncle Albert stared back at her, smiling. She felt her eyelids get heavy. The next thing she knew, she was blinking and Uncle Albert was tugging on one of her braids. "Gotcha!" he said, grinning.

Casey had to grin back. Uncle Albert hadn't blinked first. Even though she knew the test was probably not foolproof, it made her feel a lot better. There was no way in the world Uncle Albert would have stolen the book! He was just too nice. Wasn't he?

Milton and Renee came back into the room. "Okay," Milton was saying to Renee. "I'll drop you off at work. Then I'll swing by the deli on the way to my appointment."

"What kind of work do you do on Sunday?" Gaby asked.

"Just business stuff," Milton said. "Nothing you girls would be interested in."

Casey shrugged. "Try us," she said. She was beginning

to find Milton annoying. He seemed to think she and Gaby were little kids or something.

Milton winked at Casey. "I'm just trying to make a little extra money, is all, so I can marry your cousin in style. Here's a tip: Start saving now, Casey-Case."

"Just *Casey*," Casey said firmly. "I don't have a nickname."

"I like this girl," Milton said to Renee. "Let's take her home with us."

"I already have a home," Casey said.

Milton laughed. "Let's get a move on, Renee," he said. "I've got business to do."

"You and all your wheeling and dealing," Renee said. "Sometimes I think you love it more than you love me."

"Never, ever!" Milton said, and kissed her cheek again.

When the door closed behind Milton and Renee, Uncle Albert leaned back in his chair. "That boy sure is on the move," he said. "A law degree and all that hustling—and besides, he's got four years in the Marine Corps!"

The Marine Corps? There was her chance. "You were in the military, right, Uncle Albert?" Casey said quickly. "Weren't you in a war?"

"Sure was," Uncle Albert replied. "Got part of my knee blown off to prove it. And it never healed. In my day, black men fought in their own regiments. Mine was the 197th Regiment, as brave and proud and strong as the 54th." He sighed.

Casey and Gaby hardly heard his last sentence. They were staring at each other. The 54th?

Casey leaned forward. "What was the 54th?" she asked.

Uncle Albert stared at her. "Child, where have you been? The 54th was the first group of black men to fight in the Civil War. Why, Frederick Douglass played a key role in getting those men fighting!" He shook his head. "Listen, the minute you all find that book of his, you'd better pick it up and read it. You have a lot to learn."

On the corner of 125th and Lenox, Casey stopped to look around for a pay phone. "I want to call home and tell the team about the 54th Regiment," she told Gaby. "Whatever that clue that Ghostwriter found means, I don't think it has anything to do with Uncle Albert."

"We still can't cross him completely off the list," Gaby reminded her. "But at least one of the clues against him is gone."

"Yeah." Casey frowned. Something was tickling at the back of her mind.

"What's wrong? You look like you just bit a lemon," Gaby said.

"I don't know." Casey shook her head. "I feel like we're missing something. Something really important."

"Like what?" Gaby said.

"That's just it," Casey answered. "I don't have a clue!"

Chapter 10

GHOSTWRITER, Hector typed on Jamal's computer. PLEASE LOOK ONE MORE TIME AROUND THE BOOK. WE NEED MORE CLUES!

ANSWERS ARE HARD TO FIND, Ghostwriter wrote back. I'LL DO MY BEST.

Hector leaned back in Jamal's desk chair and cracked his knuckles. "I like being a detective," he said. "Especially when it means I get to work on your computer, Jamal."

Jamal smiled. "Come over any time," he said.

Just then the doorbell rang. "That's got to be Lenni and Tina," Jamal said. He and Hector bounded down the steps to the front door.

"Sailing," Lenni announced when Jamal opened the door. " 'Naut. mi.' is short for 'nautical mile' and it's a measurement for sailing."

She and Tina came inside. Jamal frowned. "So what does the clue mean?"

"We don't know," Tina said. "But we have an idea. 'Hispaniola' sounds like the name of a place. Maybe someone is sailing there."

Jamal shrugged. "I never heard of that place. Let's look it up in the atlas."

"The what?" Hector asked.

"The atlas," Jamal repeated. He crossed to the bookshelf that covered one whole wall of the living room and pulled down a big book. "Here it is. It's a book of maps. Like an encyclopedia of the world."

"My dad has one in his car," Lenni chimed in. "It helps us figure out where we're going on road trips." She laughed. "But he still gets lost all the time."

Jamal opened the big book and thumbed through it.

"Hey, that's cool," Hector said, peering over Jamal's shoulder. "But how's a person going to find one tiny place? There must be thousands of countries in there."

"And cities, and states, and provinces," Tina said, nodding.

"It's not so hard," Jamal said. He turned to the back of the book. "You have to look in the index. Everything is listed alphabetically."

Lenni was also leaning over Jamal's shoulder. "There it is," she said. "Hispaniola, page 65."

Jamal turned to page 65. "Hey!" Hector cried. "It's a

map of the West Indies. Look, there's Puerto Rico! That's where I'm from!"

"And there's Hispaniola, right nearby," Jamal said. "It's an island that Haiti and the Dominican Republic share." He bent over the map, studying it.

"That's why Alex thought the name sounded Spanish," Lenni suggested. "They speak Spanish in the Dominican Republic."

Tina pulled out the casebook. "Okay, so now we know—what?"

"Aha!" Jamal cried suddenly. "We know one more thing!" He pointed at the map. "Look at these lines of longitude and latitude."

"Whatitude and whatitude?" Hector murmured.

"These lines here." Jamal pointed at some straight, thin lines on the map. Some of them ran from left to right, and others ran from top to bottom. "They help you figure out where on the map you are. See how they're numbered? The ones that run up and down tell you where you are, north or south, and the ones that run from left to right tell you where you are, east or west." He tapped the map with his finger. "And look at these numbers right at Hispaniola. Twenty degrees north, and sixty-four degrees west."

"Those are the same numbers Ghostwriter brought us," Tina said, showing everyone the casebook.

Jamal nodded. "I bet you Ghostwriter was reading off a map. A map of Hispaniola."

The four team members sat silently for a minute. Then Hector shook his head. "Okay, so Ghostwriter was reading from a map. But I don't get it," he said. "I still don't see what the clue means."

"Neither do I," Jamal admitted. He struck his fist down on the map. "Why can't we get anywhere on this case? None of these clues mean anything!"

"Jamal, we'll get the book back," Lenni told him. "Did you call the deli delivery guy yet?"

"I was just about to, when you guys got here." Jamal stood up. "Come on into the kitchen. I'll do it now."

He looked up Simon's Deli in the telephone book. "Simmons . . . Simms . . . Simon's!" he said. "Here it is." He punched in the number on the wall phone. After four rings, someone answered. "Simon's Deli."

"Hi," Jamal said nervously. "I was wondering about deliveries."

"No deliveries today," the voice said. "My delivery boy quit."

Jamal's stomach sank. "Quit?"

"Walked in this morning, told me he was out of here, and left," the man said. "Not even a goodbye."

"What was his name?" Jamal asked. "Do you know how I can reach him?"

"I guess you really want a sandwich, huh?" the man said. "His name was Albert Fine. When you see him, tell him don't even bother to pick up his last paycheck. Say, kid, you looking for a job?"

"No, thanks," Jamal said, and hung up quickly. He turned to his friends. "Guys, he has to be our thief!" he said. "Get this—his name is Albert!"

"Albert? Like 'your loving Albert'?" Lenni said. Her eyes were wide. "Oh, wow, too much!"

Jamal slapped his forehead as he remembered something else. "I should have guessed. His shirt had the name 'Al' stenciled on it," he said. "We could have saved ourselves some running around."

"Well, we know now," Tina pointed out. "What should we do next?"

"He quit his job today," Jamal reported. "I'm going to see if I can reach him at home." He reached for the White Pages. "Oh, no! There must be a hundred Fines listed here!" He groaned. "And at least twenty of them are Alberts."

Lenni reached for the phone book and began copying numbers out of it. "I have six quarters," she said. "I'll try these first six numbers at the pay phone on the corner." She hurried out.

"I'll read the numbers to you," Hector said to Jamal. "Just relax and dial, okay?"

Jamal had to smile. "Okay."

The first four numbers rang and rang without anyone answering. When Jamal dialed the fifth number, a garbled recording came on.

"Anything?" Tina whispered.

Jamal put his finger to his lips. Then he shook his head. "The number is disconnected," he said, and hung up. "Next number, please, Hector."

This time there was a click after the second ring. Then a recorded voice came on. "Hi, this is Albert."

Jamal recognized it immediately. "It's him!" he whispered. "On a recording."

"I'm out of town for a while," the recording went on, "but you can still leave messages here for my roommate, Mike Melman. . . ."

Jamal wasn't listening any more. He felt as though his heart had stopped. Slowly he hung up the phone.

"What's wrong?" Tina asked.

"He left town," Jamal said hollowly. "Guys, what if Albert Fine stole our book—and now he's on his way to Hispaniola with it?"

"Oh, no," Hector groaned. "We'll *never* get it back!"

Chapter 11

Just then the doorbell rang again. Tina ran to get it. She came back into the kitchen with Lenni two steps behind her. "Negative," Lenni said. "Negative, negative."

"It doesn't matter," Tina said. She quickly explained to Lenni what Jamal had learned.

"Whoa." Lenni sank down on one of the kitchen chairs. "What are we going to do?"

"Let's call the police in Hispaniola and tell them to arrest Albert Fine when he gets off his sailboat!" Hector suggested.

"I don't think they'd listen to us," Jamal said glumly.

"Hey," Tina said. "Ghostwriter's back!"

Ghostwriter's glow was moving across the casebook, which was lying open on the kitchen table. In a moment a message appeared:

I'M A REALLY NICE GUY AND I'M HERE TO SAY
I WONDER IF YOU'D BE MINE TODAY?
IF YOU SAY YES, WE CAN GO AWAY

Tina copied it down, then read the words aloud. "It sounds like a rap," she said. "Or part of one."

"Weak!" Jamal said.

"I could write a better rap standing on my head," Lenni added. She and Jamal laughed and slapped hands.

"You guys," Tina said. "I think it's part of a love letter. And it's romantic!"

"Ugh." Hector made a face.

"A love letter?" Jamal hooted. Then suddenly he stopped laughing. "Hey, wait." He pulled the casebook toward him. "A love letter . . . "

"What about a love letter?" Lenni asked impatiently.

"There was a love letter in the book," Jamal said. "In fact, there were lots of them. All sent to my great-great-grandmother." He squinted, trying to remember. "How did it go? I remember it was all full of weird abbreviations and funny ways of saying things. . . . Oh! I remember how it started." He uncapped his pen and said the words out loud as he wrote them down.

My dearest Beatrice,
Thank you for yr. letter. I am keeping well though
on Thsdy. last (20th Jnry.) I suffered a touch of the
grippe.

"Weird," Lenni said softly. "It sounds like it's from a
hundred years ago."

Hector was peering at the page. "Hey," he said. "Look
at the way whoever wrote this spelled 'your.' Y, R. It's a
. . . a what-do-you call it . . . a contraction."

"So are 'Thsdy' and 'Jnry,' " Tina said. "They're short
for 'Thursday' and 'January.' "

"Yeah, but that's not what I meant," Hector said. He
looked excited. "We had another clue with contractions in
it. 'Yr lovg Albt.' Remember?"

"Hey," Jamal breathed.

Lenni's eyes went round. "Are you thinking . . . that
the person who wrote 'Yr lovg Albt'—"

"Is the same as the person that wrote that love letter to
Beatrice," Hector finished, nodding. "Maybe Ghostwriter
was reading out of one of the love letters in the book."

At that moment they heard the front door open. A
second later Grandma CeCe came into the kitchen, both
hands full of shopping bags.

"Hey, everyone," Grandma said. "Why are you sitting

around looking so down? I think you all need more sunshine. Makes you feel good."

"Grandma," Jamal said. "You remember that old love letter we read yesterday? The one that was inside the Frederick Douglass book?"

Grandma thought for a moment while she poured herself some iced tea. Then she nodded. "Albert's letter to Grandma Beatrice."

"Wait a second," Lenni said. "How could your grandmother be in love with Jamal's Uncle Albert?"

Grandma threw back her head and laughed out loud. "You kids *do* need some sun! My grandmother Beatrice was in love with her husband, Albert Darden." She looked at Jamal. "The one she called 'Mr. Darden,' like I told you. That's who my brother Albert was named for."

Jamal, Lenni, Tina, and Hector all stared at each other. Their mouths were hanging open.

"Another Albert?" Hector moaned. "That makes three!"

Grandma CeCe didn't hear him. "Beatrice must have been so in love with that man. . . . She saved every letter he ever wrote her." Grandma's voice grew softer. "They were all she had to remember him. My grandfather was sailing to Haiti when his ship disappeared. Grandma Beatrice never heard from him again."

"Haiti?" Tina whispered. "That's part of Hispaniola!"

Grandma CeCe sighed. "Well, that's all ancient history now. Happened before I was born—before my mother was born, in fact. It's just a story now, gets passed down generation to generation." She sighed again and stood up. "Let me get this old body in gear. Bought some sheets and towels today at a white sale. I'm going upstairs to put them away."

When she was gone Hector pressed his hands to his head. "My brain is starting to hurt," he complained. "What does all this mean?"

"Here's what I think it means," Tina said. She pulled the casebook toward her and put a line through 'Yr lovg Albt' and 'Hispaniola   300 naut. mi.' "I think we've been on the wrong track with some of the clues Ghostwriter found."

"Yeah," Jamal agreed. "I think he must have been reading from stuff that was in the book. 'Yr lovg Albt' was in one of the letters that my great-great-grandfather wrote to my great-great grandmother."

"And the stuff about Hispaniola was maybe from a map she had that showed where he was going," Lenni put in. "Maybe he sent it to her to show her where he was."

"Hector, if you hadn't noticed that the 'yr' in the part of the letter that I remembered was the same as the 'yr' in the clue that Ghostwriter brought back, we might never have figured all this out," Jamal said.

Hector beamed. "Thanks—even if I didn't get what you just said!"

"Okay, let's rewind. What do we know?" Tina said.

"Boy, is Alex going to be sorry he missed all this," Hector murmured.

"We know that 'Yr lovg Albt' and 'Hispaniola' don't have anything to do with my Uncle Albert—" Jamal said.

"Or Albert Fine, the deli guy," Lenni put in.

"Right." Jamal nodded. "Those clues don't tell us anything, because we know they were written by my great-great-grandfather. And, obviously, *he* couldn't have stolen the book, because he disappeared a zillion years ago!"

"Do you think your great-great-grandfather wrote that weak rap?" Tina asked suddenly.

Lenni frowned. "I don't think he could have. Rap wasn't even invented back then, was it?" she said.

"Hey, that's true," Jamal said. "So maybe that rap really is a clue."

The four gathered around the casebook and studied the poem again. After a moment Hector shook his head. "All I know is, whoever wrote it will never win a Grammy award."

Just then the phone rang. Jamal jumped to get it.

"Jamal," came Casey's voice. "Gaby and I are still up in Harlem. We're in the train station, but the train is being slow—there was a track fire or something."

"We figured out some stuff," Jamal began.

"So did we!" Casey bubbled. "Guess what? The 54th Regiment was the first black battalion."

"Did Uncle Albert fight in it?" Jamal asked.

"He would have to be ancient," Casey replied. "It was during the Civil War."

"All right!" Jamal crowed. "Negative?"

"Negative," Casey agreed.

Jamal pulled the casebook over and drew a line through "54TH REGIMENT." Then he stared at the book. "Hey, all *right*," he exclaimed. "Casey, that was the last clue against Uncle Albert! He's off the hook!"

Quickly Jamal brought his cousin up to date on what the team had learned from Grandma CeCe.

"Hooray!" Casey cheered. Then she paused for a second. "But where do we go from here?"

"Well." Jamal glanced at Tina, Lenni, and Hector. "I think Albert Fine is still the best suspect. Okay, he isn't 'yr lovg Albt' and he's probably not on his way to Hispaniola, but there's still that writing from Simon's Deli that Ghostwriter found." He consulted the casebook again.

"You know—'uper club, five ninety-five'? I mean, who else would have something like that lying around?"

There was a long silence on the other end of the line.

"Casey?" Jamal said. "Casey, are you still there?" His stomach lurched. She and Gaby were in Harlem by themselves. Were they okay?

Suddenly Casey let out an ear-splitting yell. *"I've got it! I've got it!"*

"Got what?" Jamal demanded. "Casey, what are you talking about?"

"I have to call you back, Jamal!" Casey screamed. "Don't move away from that phone!"

"Casey!"

But the line went dead.

Chapter 12

"Gaby!" Casey said. "Come on! I just remembered something!"

"What?" A train was just pulling into the station. Gaby had to yell over the noise. "Casey, this is our train. We've been waiting forever for it. And my parents will kill me if I don't get home before dark!"

"It's an emergency. Come on!" Casey grabbed Gaby's hand and pulled her down the platform. All the while, she was talking almost faster than Gaby could follow.

"At the reunion, Renee said that Milton's favorite sandwich was a ham, horseradish, and pickle club."

"Yuck!" Gaby said, making a face.

"Double yuck," Casey agreed. "But just now, when we were at Uncle Albert's, Milton kept talking about how he wanted another of those sandwiches. And he called it a Super Club, remember? And he said it cost five ninety-five."

"Yeah," Gaby puffed. The two girls ran up the steps to the street. "So?"

"Well, the writing about the deli that Ghostwriter found said 'uper club, five ninety-five,' " Casey said. "Don't you think that could have been 'super club'? Only the paper got torn so the first letter was missing."

"But the paper was from Simon's Deli, and that's in Brooklyn," Gaby objected. "Milton lives in Harlem. Do you really think he'd go all the way to Brooklyn for a sandwich?"

"No," Casey said. She smiled triumphantly. "But there *is* a Simon's in Harlem. Right on East 125th Street. Don't you remember those two addresses at the bottom? And Jamal saying he didn't know they had another store in Harlem?"

"Oh! Yeah!" Gaby's eyes grew round. "So maybe the paper from Simon's Deli that Ghostwriter found—"

"Was in Milton's house!" Casey finished. "Along with our book!"

"Casey, you're a genius," Gaby said solemnly.

"Thank you, thank you. No applause, please," Casey said.

"So where are we going now?" Gaby asked as they hurried along 125th Street.

"To Simon's," Casey replied. "Maybe Milton will still be there. And then . . . " She clenched her fists. "Then we'll make him give us back our book!"

"Jamal, who was that on the phone?" Grandma CeCe asked, coming into the kitchen. Then she frowned. "And where's that Casey?"

"Uh . . . " Jamal ducked his head. "That was Casey on the phone," he said.

"Oh, really? Where was she calling from?"

"Harlem," Jamal mumbled.

Grandma sat down at the table, picking up her empty lemonade glass. "Where? I didn't hear you, sugar."

Jamal cleared his throat. "Harlem," he said a little louder. "She—uh—went to visit Uncle Albert after we all went to Aunt Estelle's."

"Harlem!" Grandma shot up from her chair. The lemonade glass slipped out of her hand and shattered on the floor.

"Let me get that," Jamal said, bounding up from his seat.

"You just stay put," Grandma ordered. "I don't want you getting cut." She went over to the closet by the refrigerator and took out the dustpan and brush. Then she put them down on the counter and faced the team, her hands on her hips. "That child is in Harlem by herself at this hour?"

"Gaby went with her," Hector volunteered.

"And just how were they planning on getting home?" Grandma demanded. She swept up the glass with long, angry strokes. Then she started to reach for the phone. "It's expensive, but I'm going to call Albert and tell him to put them in a cab."

"Uh—she isn't at Uncle Albert's," Jamal said. "She was calling from the subway."

"The *subway!?*" Grandma cried. She stared at Jamal. "Jamal, how could you let her go off by herself like that? How could you be so irresponsible?"

Jamal hung his head. So did Lenni, Tina, and Hector. They all felt terrible. What if Casey and Gaby were really in danger?

"We never should have let them go by themselves," Tina whispered. "We should have gone with them."

Just then the phone rang again. Jamal jumped to answer it.

"It's me," Casey said.

"Casey, you'd better find a taxi and get home right now. Grandma will pay," Jamal said. "She's really—"

"Listen!" Casey interrupted. "I solved the mystery!"

"You did?" Jamal said, astonished.

"Yep," Casey said proudly. "I figured out—without anybody else's help, thank you very much—that the piece of paper from Simon's with the sandwich order on it was Milton's. 'Uper club' is really a *Super* Club—and the Super Club is Milton's favorite sandwich! And get this!" Casey's voice got higher with excitement. "Gaby and I just went to the 125th Street branch of Simon's Deli. We were hoping to catch Milton there."

"Did you?" Jamal demanded.

"Well, no," Casey admitted. "We missed him—he had just left. But the man behind the counter told us that when Milton came to pick up his sandwich, he had a small leather book with him that he was really excited about. And he said he had some business to take care of at Jameson's Antiques and Collectibles, and would they please hurry up with his sandwich! He's going to sell our book. I know it! We're going there now to find him. You have to come meet us! And bring the whole team. Here's the address."

"Wait," Jamal said. He grabbed a pencil and the casebook. "Okay, go ahead." He wrote the address down as Casey gave it to him.

"Hurry, Jamal," Casey said. "Hurry!"

Chapter 13

"Is that child crazy?" Grandma CeCe groaned, when Jamal told her where Casey was. He had decided it was better not to say *why*. "I ought to . . . "

"Grandma, don't worry. She'll be okay. I'm going to meet her," Jamal said. He looked at the other team members. "Can you guys come, too?"

"Let me call my parents," Tina said.

"And I should tell my dad," Lenni added.

Hector was already at the front door. "I'm going to get Alex!" he called. "We'll meet you there. Don't do anything without us!"

While Tina and Lenni called their parents, Jamal went over to Grandma CeCe. "I'm sorry," he said. "I know I shouldn't have let Casey and Gaby go off alone. I promise it will never happen again."

"I sure hope not," Grandma said. "I'm disappointed in

you, Jamal. And I'm going with you, just to be sure everyone gets home safely."

"Grandma . . . " Jamal said.

"Don't 'Grandma' me. Just let me get my purse."

Grandma hurried out of the kitchen. Jamal looked at Lenni and Tina and sighed.

"I think I'd better tell her the whole story on the way," he said.

Lenni nodded. "Maybe if she knows we've been trying to get back the Frederick Douglass book, you won't be in so much trouble."

"Right," Jamal said. "I won't be killed. I'll just be grounded for the next fifty years!"

"This place is creepy," Gaby said nervously.

She and Casey were standing in front of a burned-out building. Beside it there was a small bodega with stands half full of sickly-looking fruit. Next to that was Jameson's Antiques and Collectibles.

It didn't look like an antique shop. Its windows were small, with bars over them, and inside there was a long glass-fronted counter full of all sorts of things, from old electric mixers to rings and necklaces. Casey had a feeling it was really a pawnshop, not an antique shop.

Casey had been to a pawnshop once in Detroit. Because they never seemed to have enough money these days, her mother had had to sell some of their stuff. The pawnshop in Detroit still had the family's toaster oven and the tiny amethyst ring Grandma CeCe had given Casey for her eighth birthday. Casey's mother had promised to buy the ring back as soon as she had a job again. Grandma hadn't asked Casey about the ring. Casey figured she must have thought it lost or stolen.

"It's almost seven-thirty," Gaby said, checking her watch. "The sign on the door says Jameson's closes at seven-thirty. Maybe Milton isn't coming tonight, Casey."

"He'll come," Casey said, trying to sound confident. She looked around. A group of men was lounging on the corner, drinking something out of brown paper bags. Across the street, a teenage boy walked slowly by, staring at the girls. She wished a police car would come by. They'd been standing in this spot for almost twenty minutes, but not a single one had driven down the block.

And it was beginning to get dark.

"What if Milton doesn't show?" Gaby asked. Her voice shook a little. "Or . . . what if he does?"

Just then Casey spotted him. He was hurrying toward the store. In his hand was a brown briefcase.

"There he is!" Casey whispered. Her heart was pounding. She and Gaby stepped back into the shadows.

"Is he going into the shop?" Gaby asked.

Casey nodded. "I wish Jamal and the team would hurry up and get here," she said tensely.

She waited another minute. Then she couldn't stand it any more. "Come on," she whispered. They sneaked up to the window of the shop and peeked in.

"It's there!" Casey gasped. "Look—he's showing it to the store owner! That's our book!"

"Shh!" Gaby whispered. "If he hears us, we're in big trouble!"

"Where *are* those guys?" Casey moaned.

Inside the store, the store owner was going slowly through the book. He kept pointing to the pages and shaking his head. Milton was looking angrier and angrier. He stamped his foot and said something in a loud voice. Casey couldn't make out the words, though.

Finally the shop owner nodded and closed the book. He moved down the counter to the cash register and began counting out bills.

"He's going to buy it! Milton's going to sell our book!" Casey practically screamed. "What are we going to do?"

"Casey! Gaby!" came Jamal's voice behind them.

The two girls spun around. Jamal, Lenni, and Tina were running toward them. Behind the team, Grandma CeCe was puffing along.

"He sold it," Casey said. "Milton just sold our book."

"Say what?" Grandma CeCe panted.

Casey grabbed Jamal and Grandma CeCe by the hand and dragged them toward the door of Jameson's. "Come on! We have to stop him before he gets away!"

"Let me handle this," Grandma said firmly. She pushed open the door and strode inside. Casey and Jamal stared at each other for a second. Then they and their friends followed her in.

Milton turned around. When he saw Grandma CeCe his eyes bugged out for a second. Then he tried on a pleasant smile. "Well, hello, Mrs. Jenkins," he said. "Isn't it a lovely evening! Fancy meeting you—"

"Is that our Frederick Douglass book there?" Grandma CeCe demanded. She pointed to the counter.

Milton's face went gray. He fumbled for words. Then, suddenly, he turned and started running for the open door.

"*Keyaii!*" Gaby screamed. She kicked her leg out into the air.

Milton tripped and went flying headlong through the door. He landed with a thud on the sidewalk outside. "Ooohh," he groaned.

"Solid!" Casey said. She and Gaby slapped hands.

People started running toward the shop. Soon a crowd surrounded Milton. He lay on the ground, groaning and clutching his arm.

At that moment a police car turned the corner and began cruising down the street. It stopped at the crowd, and a young officer climbed out.

"What's going on here?" he asked. His face was friendly and bright. Casey sighed with relief. It was over!

Grandma CeCe stepped forward and started explaining things to the officer. The team gathered around and gazed down at Milton.

"Why?" Jamal asked him. "Why'd you steal our book?"

"I needed the money," Milton said in a low voice. He looked as if he were about to cry. "I had debts I needed to pay—fast. There were some people who were hounding me for cash. It seemed like a fast way to solve all my problems."

"But our family history was in that book!" Casey said. "How could you take it away from us?"

"I was going to buy it back for you as soon as I could," Milton said. "As soon as my law career got off the ground. As soon as Renee and I were married." He sniffled. "She won't marry me now. She'd never want a jailbird."

"She also won't want someone who stole from her family," Jamal told him. "Milton, for a guy who's supposed to be so smart, you did a pretty dumb thing."

Milton nodded and stared at the sidewalk.

"Coming through, coming through," a familiar voice called behind them. Casey, Jamal, Gaby, Lenni, and Tina turned around. Hector and Alex were pushing through the crowd.

"Hey, everybody!" Alex said breathlessly. "Did we miss anything?"

Chapter 14

"And look at this," Jamal said. He held up a yellowed piece of paper. " 'Abraham Steward—Company E—Massachussets 54th Regiment.' It's an honorable discharge from the army."

It was a few days later. The whole team was gathered around the kitchen table at the Jenkins house, poring over the family mementos from the *Narrative of the Life of Frederick Douglass*.

"So one of your ancestors was in the first black regiment," Alex said.

"Yeah, and he fought in the Civil War," Hector added. "That's so cool!"

"Milton said when he took the book home with him, he pulled all the family stuff out of it," Casey told the team. "He thought it would be easier to sell—and harder to trace—if it didn't have all that extra stuff about us in it.

Grandma and Uncle Albert went to Milton's apartment to get it all back. It was spread out all over his desk."

"So that's why Ghostwriter was bringing back all those weird clues," Lenni said. "He was reading your family mementos, which were lying around the book."

Jamal laughed. "Yeah, well, apparently Milton also took the time to read up on our family history. He wanted to know all about Renee's background." He snapped his fingers. "Hey, that reminds me. You know, there was one clue Ghostwriter brought us that we never figured out. Remember that rap?"

"Ugh," Lenni said. "How could we forget?"

"Guess who wrote it?" Jamal said. "Milton."

"Milton?" Gaby nearly choked on a cookie. "You mean he's a poet on the side?"

"Not exactly. But at the reunion, Renee said that when Milton asked her to marry him, he proposed without a single spoken word," Jamal said. "Remember, Casey?"

"Oh, yeah," Casey said. "So you mean . . ."

"Yeah," Jamal said. "I mean he wrote that rap for her. Ghostwriter found one of the rough drafts mixed in with all those other papers on Milton's desk."

Gaby shook her head. "Maybe you should worry about your cousin Renee, you guys. When she read that awful rap, she should have *known* Milton was no good!"

Everyone laughed. Then Casey spoke up.

"Well, I guess Milton learned his lesson," she said. "Grandma decided not to press charges. After all, we did get the book and the stuff inside back, no harm done. And Renee broke off the engagement. Grandma thinks that's enough punishment for one love-struck man."

"Hey, what about that deli delivery guy?" Tina said suddenly. "Did anyone ever find out why he quit his job and disappeared like that?"

"Yeah, I did," Jamal said. "I saw him playing basketball in the park yesterday." He grinned. "You know why he left town so fast? He had to go up to Boston, because he had just gotten a phone call from Harvard. They wanted to talk to him about giving him a scholarship to study history!"

"A scholarship? You mean they're going to pay him to do all that reading and stuff?" Hector asked, amazed. "Wow, that's incredible."

Just then Danitra came into the kitchen. She was carrying a photo that had been taken at the reunion. In it, she, Jamal, and Casey were sitting on the couch. Behind them stood Mr. and Mr. Jenkins, Grandma CeCe, Aunt Estelle, and Uncle Albert. Everyone was smiling happily into the camera.

Casey took the photo from Danitra and placed it between the pages of the old book. "There."

"Now we're complete," Jamal said.

"Don't be so sure," Danitra warned. "You never know when a tall, handsome stranger in a dashiki is going to come along and sweep me off my feet!"

"Just so long as he isn't another Milton," Casey said.

Danitra laughed and went into the living room.

Lenni turned another page of the book and pulled out an ancient-looking map of Hispaniola. "Hispaniola—300 nautical miles," she said, tracing the old pencil marks with her finger. "What do you think happened to Albert Darden?"

Casey shrugged. "Maybe he's still out there, somewhere."

"Ooh, Casey," Tina said. "That's so *romantic*!"

At that moment Ghostwriter's glow swept over the open pages of the book. HISTORY HAS BEEN RESTORED, he wrote. THAT'S GOOD!

Casey took the pen from around her neck and grabbed a piece of scrap paper. THANKS TO YOU, GW, she wrote back. IF IT HADN'T BEEN FOR YOU AND THOSE WEIRD CLUES, WE'D NEVER HAVE GOTTEN THE BOOK BACK. AND THEN WE WOULDN'T HAVE LEARNED ALL ABOUT OUR FAMILY!

Ghostwriter's glow seemed to get a little brighter for a moment. Then he wrote: HOW MUCH DID THE MAN IN THE ANTIQUE STORE SAY THE BOOK WAS WORTH?

Casey smiled. HE DIDN'T SAY, she answered. BUT I KNOW. IT'S ABSOLUTELY PRICELESS.

From the Hit TV Show

GHOST writer

Created by CTW

BECOME AN OFFICIAL
GHOSTWRITER READERS CLUB MEMBER!

You'll receive the following GHOSTWRITER Readers Club Materials:
Official Membership Card • The Scoop on GHOSTWRITER •
GHOSTWRITER Magazine
All members registered by December 31st will have a chance to win
a FREE COMPUTER and other exciting prizes!

OFFICIAL ENTRY FORM

Mail your completed entry to: Bantam Doubleday Dell BFYR,
GW Club, 1540 Broadway, New York, NY 10036

Name _____

Address _____

City _____ **State** _____ **Zip** _____

Age _____ **Phone** _____

Club Sweepstakes Official Rules

1. No purchase necessary. Enter by completing and returning the Entry Coupon. All entries must be received by Bantam Doubleday Dell no later than December 31, 1993. No mechanically reproduced entries allowed. By entering the sweepstakes, each entrant agrees to be bound by these rules and the decision of the judges which shall be final and binding. Limit: one entry per person.

2. The prizes are as follows: Grand Prize: One computer with monitor (approximate retail value of Grand Prize $3,000), First Prizes: Ten GHOSTWRITER libraries (approximate retail value of each First Prize: $25), Second Prizes: Five GHOSTWRITER backpacks (approximate retail value of each Second Prize: $25), and Third Prizes: Ten GHOSTWRITER T-Shirts (approximate retail value of each Third Prize: $10). Winners will be chosen in a random drawing on or about January 10, 1994, from among all completed Entry Coupons received and will be notified by mail. Odds of winning depend on the number of entries received. No substitution or transfer of the prize is allowed. All entries become property of BDD and will not be returned. Taxes, if any, are the sole responsibility of the winner. BDD reserves the right to substitute a prize of equal or greater value if any prize becomes unavailable.

3. This sweepstakes is open only to the residents of the U.S. and Canada, excluding the Province of Quebec, who are between the ages of 6 and 14 at the time of entry. The winner, if Canadian, will be required to answer correctly a time-limited arithmetical skill testing question in order to receive the prize. Employees of Bantam Doubleday Dell Publishing Group Inc. and its subsidiaries and affiliates and their immediate family members are not eligible. Void where prohibited or restricted by law. Grand and first prize winners will be required to execute and return within 14 days of notification an affidavit of eligibility and release to be signed by winner and winner's parent or legal guardian. In the event of noncompliance with this time period, an alternate winner will be chosen.

4. Entering the sweepstakes constitutes permission for use of the winner's name, likeness, and biographical data for publicity and promotional purposes on behalf of BDD, with no additional compensation. For the name of the winner, available after January 31, 1994, send a self-addressed envelope, entirely separate from your entry, to Bantam Doubleday Dell, BFYR Marketing Department, 1540 Broadway, New York, NY 10036.